# The Christmas Angel

# The Christmas Angel

## HANS WILHELM

Little
Shepherd
BOOKS™

an imprint of
SCHOLASTIC INC.

New York  Toronto  London  Auckland  Sydney
Mexico City  New Delhi  Hong Kong  Buenos Aires

There was great excitement in Heaven. The angels had learned that the Son of God would soon be born in the little town of Bethlehem. He would be called Jesus.

The news spread from cloud to cloud. "We are going down to Earth to welcome the baby!" The smallest angel was the most excited of all.

"I will bring the baby a present," the little angel said.

But what kind of gift could he bring? He didn't have anything that would be good enough for the Son of God. He thought and thought. Finally, he had an idea.

"I am going to make up a song for Him!"

Now, the little angel had never made up a song before. But that didn't stop him. "The song will come from my heart," he said.

The little angel began to hum a tune. In no time at all, he had finished his song.

Baby Divine, King from on High,
I came to sing you a lullaby.
I bring you this gift on the day of your birth.
Now I can go home. I found Heaven on Earth.

Then he ran to join the other angels. They were just getting ready to leave.

"Wait!" his guardian angel said. "I am sorry, but we cannot let you come with us. Look at your wings. They are much too small for such a long journey."

The little angel burst into tears. "That isn't fair," he cried. "I want to see the Son of God, too."

The big angels lifted up their wings and rose above the clouds. "Don't cry, little one," his guardian angel called out. "We will tell you all about it when we return. Be careful while we are gone. Don't go too close to the edge of the clouds!"

Then they flew off.

The little angel couldn't believe it. "How could they leave me behind?" he sobbed.

After a while, the little angel started to feel lonely.

He thought it must be time for the others to come back.

He walked to the very edge of a cloud to see if they were coming.

The next thing he knew, he was tumbling down, down towards Earth!

He moved his little wings back and forth, but they were not strong enough to stop his fall.

Closer and closer to Earth he came, until . . .

. . . he was caught by the branch of an old tree.

Luckily, the little angel wasn't hurt. But it was so cold!

The angel wrapped his arms around himself and thought about the warmth of Heaven, which he had become so used to.

Then he saw something that cheered him up. Off in the distance, hidden behind some olive trees, stood a tent. "It must be warm inside that tent," he thought. And he made his way through the olive trees.

The little angel peeked inside the tent. In the dim light he could see shapes. Some of the biggest shapes were men asleep on the ground. The other shapes were bags and bundles of all sorts.

"These men must be travelers," the little angel thought.
"They must be very tired if they are sleeping during the day."
At his feet, the angel saw a large soft bag that looked nice
and warm. He opened the bag and looked inside.

"What could this be?" the angel wondered.

Even in the dim light he could see brightly colored stones glowing red, green, and gold.

"A treasure!" he thought. "Who are these travelers? Could they be jewel thieves?" The little angel suddenly felt very frightened.

Just then he heard a sound. The men were waking up! Quickly, the little angel crawled into the bag and closed it.

It was not very comfortable inside the bag, but at least it was warm.

A short time later, the angel found himself on the back of a camel. The men had packed up their tent and their belongings and were on their way to — where?

The little angel didn't know. He peeked out of the bag and saw a starry sky above him.

With every step the camel took, the bag swayed and bounced. The little angel was being tumbled about like a ship in a storm.

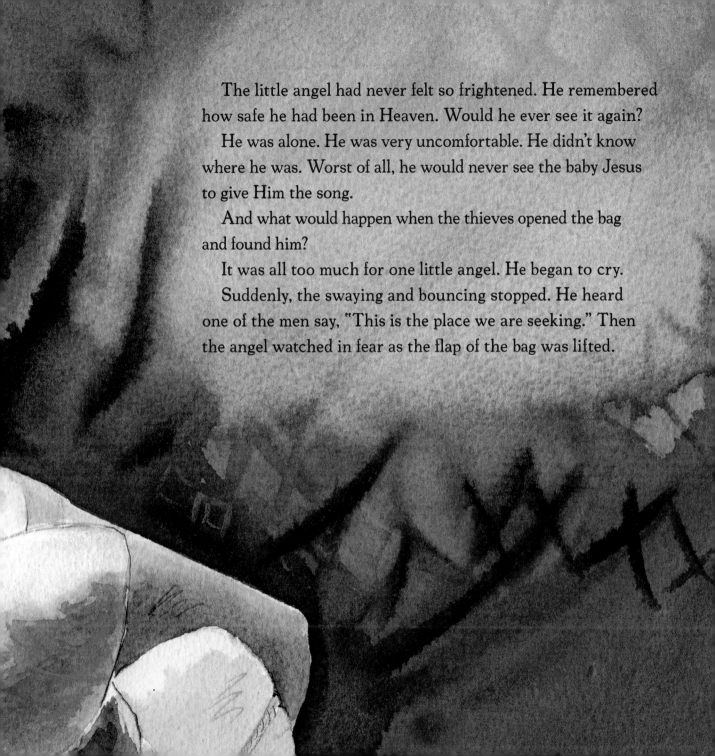

The little angel had never felt so frightened. He remembered how safe he had been in Heaven. Would he ever see it again?

He was alone. He was very uncomfortable. He didn't know where he was. Worst of all, he would never see the baby Jesus to give Him the song.

And what would happen when the thieves opened the bag and found him?

It was all too much for one little angel. He began to cry.

Suddenly, the swaying and bouncing stopped. He heard one of the men say, "This is the place we are seeking." Then the angel watched in fear as the flap of the bag was lifted.

Three very surprised faces were looking at him.

"This is a wonder to behold!" one of the men exclaimed as he lifted the angel out of the bag.

"It must be another sign of the miracle that has happened," said another. "Come, we must make ourselves ready. We will bring the little one with us."

The little angel was so relieved! These men were not thieves at all. He still did not know who they were or where he was, but he knew everything would be all right.

The men took richly colored robes out of their bags and put them on. On their heads they placed crowns of gold and jewels.

One of the men took the little angel by the hand and led him to the doorway of a small stable.

"Oh! Oh!" the little angel said when he saw the sight before him.

The stable was full of light cast by the halos of a host of angels. Shepherds with their staffs were kneeling in front of a man and woman whose faces glowed with joy as they looked down at a manger filled with straw. In the manger lay a tiny baby.

It was God's own Son, Jesus.

Very slowly, the angel walked over to the manger.
When he was next to the baby, he began to sing.

When the song was done, the baby Jesus smiled.
The smile told the little angel that Jesus knew the
song had come from his heart.

Baby Divine, King from on High,
I came to sing you a lullaby.
I bring you this gift on the day of your birth.
Now I can go home. I found Heaven on Earth.

Later, the little angel was carried
back home.

"Jesus liked my song," he said.
"I'm sure He did."

Then, with a happy smile, the little angel
fell asleep.

**HANS WILHELM** is the author and illustrator of 200 books for children and adults with more than 35 million copies in print. His books have won numerous international awards and prizes such as the prestigious Gold Medallion Book Award of the Evangelical Christian Publishers Association. His other two Little Shepherd books are *The Lord Is My Shepherd* and *Jesus Wants Me for a Sunbeam.*

The author wishes to acknowledge the contribution of Charlotte Ann Lanham, who knew the perfect words for the little angel's song.

Published by Scholastic Inc. SCHOLASTIC, LITTLE SHEPHERD BOOKS, and associated logos are trademarks and/or registered trademarks of Scholastic Inc.

ISBN-13: 978-0-545-00853-2
ISBN-10: 0-545-00853-0

12 11 10 9 8 7 6 5 4 3 2 1          7 8 9 10 11 12/0

Printed in the U.S.A.
First Scholastic paperback printing, October 2007